For Steven and Steven, with love

— B.B.

For all the fierce folks, young and old

— N.C.

Text copyright © 2019 by Bea Birdsong
Illustrations copyright © 2019 by Nidhi Chanani
Published by Roaring Brook Press
Roaring Brook Press is a division of Holtzbrinck Publishing Holdings Limited Partnership
175 Fifth Avenue, New York, NY 10010
mackids.com

Library of Congress Control Number: 2018955876

ISBN: 978-1-250-29508-8

Our books may be purchased in bulk for promotional, educational, or business use.
Please contact your local bookseller or the Macmillan Corporate and Premium Sales Department
at (800) 221-7945 ext. 5442 or by email at MacmillanSpecialMarkets@macmillan.com.

First edition, 2019
Book design by Andrew Arnold
Printed in China by Hung Hing Off-set Printing Co. Ltd., Heshan City, Guangdong Province

1 3 5 7 9 10 8 6 4 2

I WILL BE FIERCE!

written by
BEA BIRDSONG

illustrated by
NIDHI CHANANI

ROARING BROOK PRESS
New York

TODAY, I WILL BE FIERCE!

I will answer the
call to adventure.

I will put on my armor.

I will fill my treasure chest.

I will go forth to explore new worlds.

TODAY, I WILL BE FIERCE!

I will take on the monsters
that stand in my way.

I will drive back
the dragons.

I will dare to walk with the giants.

I will charge the
many-headed serpent.

TODAY, I WILL BE FIERCE!

I will chart my own course.

I will climb the
Mountain of Knowledge.

I will trick the Guardian of Wisdom
into revealing her secrets.

I will solve the
Mysteries of the Unknown.

SUNNY
WHY LOVE
WORRY NOT
SILVER TOOTH & HER ADVENTURES
MR. LOVEDUCK
THE TRUE STAR
LALO
CLEAN MAGIC
PENNIES FOR JUNE
YOUR PEN
CAPTAIN KID
UNICORN BANDIT
CADA VEZ
COLORES
ES POR TI
COUNTRY DAISY
POPPY PRINCE VOL. 1
MY SISTER'S SONG
FIRST SECOND
FUSE
SUMMER CHILD
PEABODY EYE
STREETLIGHT MOUSE
WISDOM WAITING
LEMON LASS
THE SLOW
WHERE'S HALMONI
PRINCESS, PRINCESS
WITCH BOY
SPACE BATTLE LUNCHTIME
THIS ONE SUMMER
HILO
THE SKY
BIG BREAD
THE ULTIMATE
KATO

I will break away
from the ordinary.

I will stand up for
my beliefs.

I will build new bridges.

I will search for light in the darkness.

TODAY, I WILL BE FIERCE!

I will claim my victory.

I will conquer my fears.

I will make my voice heard.

I will be the hero
of my story.

TODAY, I WILL BE FIERCE!

I will lead
the way home.

And then, I will rest.

For tomorrow,
I will be fierce again.